THE AMAZING ADVENTURES OF THE DC SUPER-PETS!

Danger in the Deep

by Steve Korté

illustrated by Mike Kunkel

PICTURE WINDOW BOOKS
a capstone imprint

Published by Picture Window Books, an imprint of Capstone
1710 Roe Crest Drive
North Mankato, Minnesota 56003
capstonepub.com

Library of Congress Cataloging-in-Publication Data
Names: Korté, Steven, author. | Kunkel, Mike, 1969- illustrator.
Korté, Steven. Amazing adventures of the DC super-pets.
Title: Danger in the deep / by Steve Korté ; illustrated by Mike Kunkel.
Description: North Mankato, Minnesota : Picture Window Books, an imprint
of Capstone, [2023] | Series: The amazing adventures of the DC super-pets
Audience: Ages 5-7. | Audience: Grades K-1. | Summary: When his friends
are captured by the evil Dr. Sivana and Dex-Starr the Red Lantern it is up
to Shazam's super pet, Hoppy the Marvel Bunny, to use his superpowers to
rescue them. Identifiers: LCCN 2022025125 (print) | LCCN 2022025126 (ebook)
ISBN 9781484672037 (hardcover) | ISBN 9781484671993 (paperback) | ISBN
9781484672006 (pdf) | ISBN 9781484675304 (kindle edition) Subjects: LCSH:
Rabbits—Juvenile fiction. | Superheroes—Juvenile fiction. | Supervillains—
Juvenile fiction. | CYAC: Rabbits—Fiction. | Superheroes—Fiction.
Supervillains—Fiction. | Ability—Fiction. Classification: LCC PZ7.K8385
Dan 2023 (print) | LCC PZ7.K8385 (ebook) | DDC [E]—dc23
LC record available at https://lccn.loc.gov/2022025125
LC ebook record available at https://lccn.loc.gov/2022025126

Designed by Elyse White

TABLE OF CONTENTS

CHAPTER 1
A Huge Hole 7

CHAPTER 2
Danger Below 15

CHAPTER 3
Catch Me If You Can 23

He is wise and courageous.

He has amazing superpowers.

He is Shazam's loyal companion.

These are . . .

THE AMAZING
ADVENTURES OF

Hoppy the
Marvel Bunny!

A Huge Hole

It is a beautiful summer day in Fawcett City. Hoppy is enjoying a picnic in the park with his good friends Millie and Tawky Tawny.

BLAM!

The sound of a powerful explosion
fills the park. The three friends look
around to see what caused the noise.

"That giant hole was not there when
we arrived," Tawky Tawny says.

Suddenly, the hero Shazam flies into

the crater!

"Let's see what is going on," says Millie.

Millie and Tawky Tawny run over to the hole.

"I'm not sure that's a good idea," says Hoppy, staying back.

"Oh, Hoppy. You're always such a scaredy-rabbit," says Millie. "What could go wrong just looking into a hole?"

Tawky Tawny leans over too far and loses his balance. He falls into the hole! "Oh no!" he shouts.

Millie yells, "We have to help Tawky Tawny!"

Millie doesn't know that Hoppy is secretly a Super Hero. Hoppy becomes the superpowered Marvel Bunny when he says the magic word Shazam!

To keep his secret, Hoppy has to pretend that he is frightened. He runs away and hides behind a tree.

"Well, it looks like it's up to me,"
says Millie, as she nervously stares
at the hole.

Millie takes a deep breath. Then she
leaps into the deep, dark hole.

Danger Below

"Shazam!" Hoppy says.

A bolt of lightning blasts above Hoppy

as he changes into Marvel Bunny.

He flies through the air and dives

into the hole.

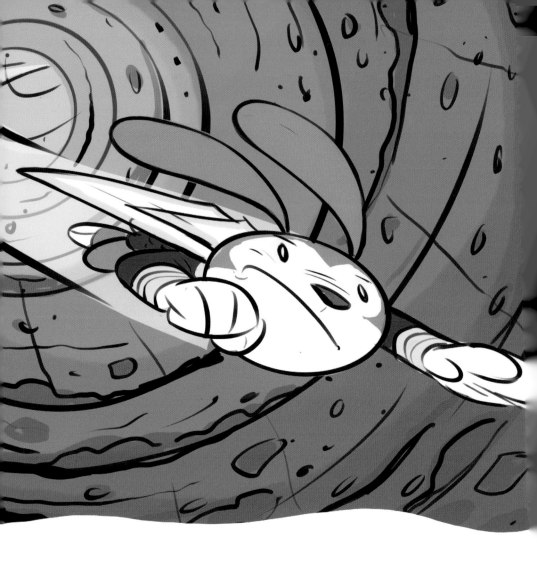

Deeper and deeper he goes. He speeds
down the long tunnel until he sees a
light. Quietly, he approaches the bottom
of the hole.

Hoppy is alarmed to see the evil scientist Dr. Sivana. He is standing near a giant cannon. The enormous weapon is pointing toward the top of the hole.

Hoppy also sees a glowing red light. It is coming from Dex-Starr, the dangerous Red Lantern cat.

The glowing red power ring on Dex-Starr's tail has created powerful ropes. They are tied tightly around Shazam, Tawky Tawny, and Millie.

"I am so pleased to have three unexpected guests here today," says Dr. Sivana. "You will be able to watch as my cannon shoots tons of stinky garbage all over Fawcett City. It will take years to clean up the mess!"

Dr. Sivana walks over to the cannon, leaving Dex-Starr to guard the three prisoners. Marvel Bunny jumps out of his hiding place.

"Here, kitty, kitty," he whispers to Dex-Starr.

Catch Me If You Can

The startled cat lets out a low growl and points its power ring toward Marvel Bunny. Marvel Bunny zooms up the tunnel. The angry cat flies in pursuit of the hero.

Suddenly, Marvel Bunny does a somersault and changes direction. The surprised cat follows him.

Just as Dex-Starr is about to catch Marvel Bunny, the hero zooms up and dodges out of the way.

Dex-Starr slams into Dr. Sivana! The collision knocks out both of the villains. The red ropes surrounding Shazam and the others disappear.

"Nice work, Marvel Bunny!" says Shazam. "Now let's take care of Sivana's cannon."

Shazam carries the villains away.
Marvel Bunny flies Millie and Tawky
Tawny up to the park.

"Oh, Marvel Bunny, you saved the
day," Millie says happily. "And once
again, that 'fraidy-rabbit Hoppy missed
all the action!"

AUTHOR!

Steve Korté is the author of many books for children and young adults. He worked at DC Comics for many years, editing more than 600 books about Superman, Batman, Wonder Woman, and the other heroes and villains in the DC Universe. He lives in New York City with his husband, Bill, and their super-cat, Duke.

ILLUSTRATOR!

Mike Kunkel wanted to be a cartoonist ever since he was a little kid. He has worked on numerous projects in animation and books, including many years spent drawing cartoon stories about creatures and super heroes such as the Smurfs and Shazam! He has won the Annie Award for Best Character Design in an Animated Television Production and is the creator of the two-time Eisner Award-winning comic book series Herobear and the Kid. Mike lives in southern California, and he spends most of his extra time drawing cartoons filled with puns, trying to learn new magic tricks, and playing games with his family.

"Word Power"

alarm (uh-LAHRM)—sudden fear

collision (kuh-LISH-uhn)—when two things run into each other

crater (KRAY-tuhr)—a large hole in the ground

dodge (DOJ)—to avoid something by moving quickly

evil (EE-vuhl)—mean or cruel

prisoner (PRIZ-uh-ner)—a person who has been caught or held for wrongdoing

pursuit (pur-SOOT)—the act of trying to obtain something

somersault (SUHM-ur-sawlt)—to roll by turning your heels over your head

unexpected (uhn-ik-SPEK-tuhd)—surprised

villain (VIL-uhn)—a wicked, evil, or bad person who is often a character in a story

WRITING PROMPTS

1. It's okay to be scared. Make a list of things you are scared of. Then write down ways you can defeat your fears.

2. Make a list of at least three excuses Hoppy can use for missing the big event.

3. Hoppy and his friends are in the park for a picnic. Write about something you like to do with your friends.

DISCUSSION QUESTIONS

1. Was it a good idea for Millie to jump in the crater after her friend? Would you do the same thing?

2. Did you like Marvel Bunny's rescue? What else could he have done to save his friends?

3. What do you think the punishment should be for Dr. Sivana and Dex-Starr?

THE AMAZING ADVENTURES OF THE DC SUPER-PETS!

Collect them all!